HOME FARM TWINS
AT STONELEA

Mac Climbs A Mountain

Home Farm Twins
at Stonelea
Mac Climbs A Mountain

Jenny Oldfield

Illustrated by Kate Aldous

*Hodder
Children's
Books*

a division of Hodder Headline

Copyright © 2000 Jenny Oldfield
Illustrations copyright © 2000 Kate Aldous

First published in Great Britain in 2000
by Hodder Children's Books

The right of Jenny Oldfield to be identified as the Author of
this Work has been asserted by her in accordance with the
Copyright, Designs and Patents Act 1988.

10 9 8 7 6 5 4 3 2 1

A Catalogue record for this book is available from the British Library

ISBN 0 340 74686 6

Typeset by Avon Dataset Ltd, Bidford-on-Avon, Warks

Printed and bound in Great Britain by
The Guernsey Press Co. Ltd, Channel Isles

Hodder Children's Books
a division of Hodder Headline
338 Euston Road
London NW1 3BH

To Tess

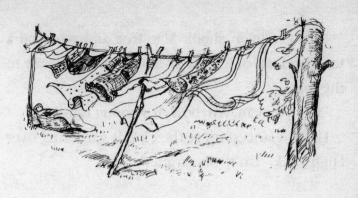

One

'Go away, Mac!' Helen cried.

She was trying to hang washing on the line and the black kitten kept grabbing the dangling corners.

'Go on, shoo!' At this rate, she would never be ready on time.

Hannah leaned out of the bedroom window. 'Get a move on, Helen! Dad'll be here soon!'

'Yeah, yeah!' So what was she supposed to do? Dump Lucy's laundry and go pack her bag? Leave little Mac to wrestle with the wet tea towels and tear the pillowcases to shreds?

'Leave that for now!' Hannah called.

'Can't!' Helen shook Mac free and whisked a tea towel out of his reach. She pegged it firmly to the line.

'Yes, you can. Anyhow, it's gonna rain!'

Helen glanced up at the clouds gathering over High Peak. 'Isn't!' she argued.

' 'Tis!'

'Isn't! Shoo, Mac . . . Mac, leggo!'

The kitten had dug his claws into one of Lucy's tablecloths and refused to let Helen hang it up.

'Look, there are dirty paw marks all over it!' She tugged harder.

Miaow-miaow-miaow! Mac hung on tight. *Good game! I like this one. Do it again!*

'Here, dear, let me do that!' a soft voice said. Lucy Carlton smiled as she came across the lawn. The old lady was dressed in a summery cream cardigan and a matching skirt. Her white hair was swept back from her thin face and held neatly in place by a pretty silver clasp.

With Mac still tugging at the cloth, Helen hesitated. 'Are you sure you can manage?'

It was only a few weeks since Lucy's accident; enough time for her injured hip to heal, but still quite soon for the Cat Lady of Stonelea to be doing normal housework.

'Look; no walking-stick!' Lucy held out her hands like a magician who has just performed a clever trick. Then she took the tablecloth from Helen. 'In any case, I'm going to have to do things for myself after you and Hannah leave.'

'I suppose so.' Reluctantly Helen handed over the task. But before she went to help Hannah with the packing, she stooped to prise Mac's claws from the end of the lacy cloth. 'Bad boy!' she scolded.

Miaow! The coal-black kitten squirmed and

3

wriggled. He turned himself round to lick Helen's face with his pink tongue.

'Hmm!' *How do you stay cross with a little cutie like Mac?* thought Helen.

'I'm going to miss you and your sister very much,' Lucy confided, as Helen tickled Mac and she continued to hang up the washing. 'You've been so good to me and my cats. I don't know what we would have done without you!'

'That's okay,' Helen muttered, then blushed. She stroked Mac under his soft, furry chin, shook his paws, scratched playfully behind his ears.

Helping out at the cat sanctuary had made the summer holidays whizz by. She and Hannah had fed the waifs and strays, rescued lost cats, taken in abandoned kittens, and loved every minute! 'We'd stay longer,' she told Lucy, 'only school starts on Monday.'

'I know, dear. And you mustn't worry about me. I'm quite fit and well again. And of course, I shan't be lonely; not with all my lovely furry friends to keep me company.'

'Helen!' Hannah leaned further out of the bedroom window and called again. 'Dad's gonna be here to pick us up in less than half an hour!'

'Coming!' Helen gave the black kitten one last tickle, then smiled wistfully at Lucy. 'I'm glad you decided to keep Mac, even though Hannah and I would've loved to have him up at Home Farm!' Along with Speckle, Solo, Socks and all the other animals that lived with them in the old farmhouse on Doveton Fell.

Putting the final peg over the corner of the tablecloth to keep it in place, the old lady smiled. 'Ah, Mac,' she sighed. 'Yes; sweet little Mac.'

'Oh, Helen!' Hannah had been the one to spot the lost kitten.

The twins had been out in Nesfield town, shopping for Lucy. They'd called in at the Curlew Café to see their mum, bought milk and bread, and were ready to cycle back out to Stonelea.

Then Hannah had heard a feeble cry coming from behind a bus shelter in the main square. She'd gone to investigate, and that was when she'd called out to her twin.

'Oh, Helen, come and look at this!'

'What now?' Helen had recognised Hannah's

tone of voice; a mixture of surprised, cross and scared. Helen called it her 'Hannah-to-the-rescue' voice. She'd propped her bike against the side of the shelter and gone round the back.

Hannah had been crouching over what looked like a big plastic paint container. It lay on its side, rolling gently in the gutter, a dribble of white paint dripping into a nearby drain. 'Take a look inside!' she'd whispered to Helen.

So Helen had got down onto her hands and knees and peered in to the plastic drum. It hadn't been empty as she'd supposed. No; something had moved. At first she hadn't been sure what it was. And the creature was crying and shivering, cowering in the bottom of the container, afraid to come out.

'It's a kitten!' Hannah had identified the tiny mewing noise. 'It's covered in paint!'

'How could anyone . . . ?' Helen had gasped and closed her eyes. The poor little thing was unrecognisable; just a sticky, bedraggled mess. She'd reached in her hand and brought the tiny creature out in to the daylight, discovering that, yes, Hannah had been right.

Mew-mew-mew! The kitten's eyes, ears and mouth had been clogged with white paint and it had been impossible to tell his true colour until Helen and Hannah had run like the wind with him across the square to the café, where their mum had quickly brought a cloth to wipe his face.

'He's black underneath all this mess!' Mary had whispered. Then, practical as ever, had told the girls not to worry. The paint was emulsion, which was water-based and so not difficult to wash off.

'Tell that to the kitten!' Helen had murmured.

He'd kept up his crying until the worst of the paint was off and Mary had wrapped him in a clean, warm towel.

'I'd like to know who did this to him!' Hannah had grown more and more angry, once she'd got over the relief of realising that the black kitten was probably going to live. 'He might've drowned in that horrible paint if the container hadn't fallen on to its side!'

'Or swallowed lots and been poisoned!' Helen had added.

'Where did you find him?' Mary had asked, now that the immediate crisis was over.

'Hannah found him behind the bus shelter.' Helen had pointed across the square. 'The paint can was lying in the gutter, just outside the door of Mac's Fish and Chip Shop!'

So they'd called him Mac.

They'd brought him out to Stonelea for Lucy to look after. Then they'd tried everything to track down the cruel person who had done this to him.

'. . . No, sorry, love.' The lady in the chip shop had shaken her head and told Hannah she was absolutely positive that the paint hadn't been spilling into the drain when she'd arrived at work at nine that morning. And no, she hadn't seen anyone dump the container. No, there was nobody employing decorators nearby.

Helen and Hannah had even asked their friend, Karl Thomas, if he knew where the paint might have come from.

Karl was a painter and decorator who lived with his wife, Sophie, and Samson, their Old English sheepdog, in Rose Terrace. 'It's a common brand of paint,' he'd told them. 'You can buy it at any do-it-yourself outlet.' He'd shrugged and been sorry that he couldn't offer more help.

It had been Lucy who had finally stopped the twins from losing too much sleep over Mac's heartless owners. 'The important thing is that the kitten has recovered from his ordeal.'

At that precise moment, Mac had been squatting ready to pounce playfully on old Sheba's twitching tail.

The elderly black cat was battle-scarred and weary from a previous life living rough. But since Lucy had taken her in to Stonelea, she'd become one of the old lady's favourites and was now a permanent fixture by the side of the warm kitchen stove.

And as soon as he'd arrived, Mac had taken to Sheba.

'Because he's a mini-version of her!' Helen had pointed out the similarities. Both Sheba and Mac were black all over. They were both rough and tough; not your refined, aloof kind of cat. Broad-chested, with wide faces and the same light green, shining eyes.

'Maybe Mac thinks Sheba's his mum!' Hannah suggested.

Mac followed Sheba wherever she went. At the end of his first day at the cat sanctuary, after Lucy had finished cleaning paint out of his black fur, Mac cheekily sidled up to the older cat at supper to share her dish. On the morning of day two, the twins came downstairs to find him curled up in her basket, with Sheba doing a spot of gentle grooming behind his ears. After a week, the cheeky kitten had become the big cat's shadow, following her every footstep.

'So I suppose I have no choice!' Lucy had declared with a mock sigh. It was two weeks after the paint incident. Hannah and Helen had had no luck with their investigations, and Mac had made himself completely at home. At that very moment, he was nestled beside Sheba on Lucy's lap. 'The little imp will have to stay!'

And now the summer holiday was over, and it was time for the twins to go home.

'Trust you to leave everything to the last minute!' Hannah complained when Helen finally hurtled into the bedroom to pack her bag.

'I couldn't help it, could I?' Helen grabbed her pyjamas and flung them into her case. Odd socks, dirty T-shirts and an old pair of trainers soon followed. 'I was hanging out the washing!'

'Looked more like you were playing with Mac to me!' Hannah sniffed. She zipped up her own neatly packed case with an efficient flick of the wrist.

Shorts, a dog-eared paperback, two sweatshirts, more odd socks . . . Helen's small case was already bursting at the seams.

'Shoo, Mac! Go away!' Hannah saw the mischievous kitten trying to sneak in through the bedroom door. She clapped her hands at him and sent him scooting out of sight.

'How long before Dad gets here?' Helen gasped, pulling a fresh bundle of crumpled clothes from under her bed. *Aaa-choo!* She sneezed in a cloud of rising dust.

'Ten minutes.' Hannah sat cross-legged in the window seat to gaze out at the garden. Washing flapped in the wind, cats strolled across the lawn, down towards the little footbridge which spanned the stream.

11

Aachoo! Aaachooo! Helen sneezed louder than before. '*Hab you seed by black drousers?*' she asked with a nose full of dust.

'No, I haven't seen your black trousers,' Hannah said airily. 'Honest, Helen, Dad'll go mad if you're not ready!'

'So?' Helen tossed her head.

'*So* . . . he has to go out again after he's collected us. And you're going to make him late.' Hannah hummed a little tune and drummed her fingers on the windowsill.

Helen found her trousers under her pillow and flung them in the case. *Aachoo!* She was just about to jump on the bag, squash the contents and close the zip when she heard a small miaow. '*Was waz dat?*'

Miaow! Louder this time. And coming from under the black trousers.

Helen held back. She flipped open the lid of the case and unearthed a wriggling ball of soft black fur. '*Mac!*' she cried.

Hannah sighed, uncrossed her legs, got down from the windowsill and went to collect the playful kitten. 'You nearly got smashed to smithereens inside Helen's case,' she cooed, putting him outside the door and watching him trot smoothly down the steep stairs. 'So, Mac, be a good boy and keep out of the way. Go on; shoo!'

Two

'It's high time we bought ourselves a new car,'
David Moore said.

Shake-rattle. Rattle-rock-shudder. The old
family saloon struggled up Hardstone Pass on the
way to Home Farm. The exhaust pipe had come
loose and was knocking against the ground every
time they hit a rough patch. The engine coughed,
spluttered and wheezed like an old man with
bronchitis.

'Yeah, like we're gonna land on Mars tomorrow!'
Helen chipped in. There was no way they could
afford to even think about buying a new car.

The twins' dad took the point. 'OK, then;

I need to devote a bit of time to fixing this one up.'

Hannah giggled. 'The same way you fixed up the old oven door when we first got to Doveton? Or the bookshelves in our bedroom, or the rabbit hutch, or . . .' She pictured spanners and oily rags scattered around the farmyard, her dad's legs poking out from underneath the old car. And half an engine laid in bits along the wall-top – springs and coils, pistons and gaskets, covered in oil and never to be put back in place.

'OK, OK!' David cleared his throat. 'Maybe I'll pop it into the garage first thing on Monday morning – just afer I've dropped you two off at *school*!'

'Yuck!'

'Ugh!' Hannah and Helen made sour-lemon faces.

'Dad, did you have to remind us?' Hannah protested. SCHOOL!

'Yeah, thanks a lot!' Helen groaned, sinking down in the back seat and glowering out at the towering slate cliffs to either side. LESSONS! Learning about the life-cycle of the gnat. Or the ground plan of the medieval fort – for the fifth time around.

'Sorry, girls!' David sang out, though he didn't sound it. In fact, he seemed pleased to have shut them up for once. He grinned at them in his overhead mirror, muttering something about snails creeping unwillingly to school.

'What are you on about?' Hannah grumbled, only half listening to the answer as she let her thoughts stray back to Stonelea. Lucy had stood at the gate to wave them off. She'd been surrounded by cats; the two fluffy Persians, Cherie and Stella, a tabby, a long-haired white and, of course, rough, tough Sheba.

'It's Shakespeare!' David replied airily. 'The seven ages of man. The schoolboy creeping unwillingly to school like a snail!'

'Wow, Dad, I'll remember that. *Not!*' Helen scoffed. In fact, the whole thing had just whooshed right over her head. Like Hannah, she was remembering their recent goodbyes.

'Bye, my dears!' Lucy had called. 'And thank you so much for all your help!'

The cats had watched the twins place their cases

in the boot of the car, sniffed around for a while, then lost interest and padded gracefully away. All except for Sheba, who had hung around until the very last minute.

In fact, Hannah had been forced to stop the black cat from climbing right into the boot.

'Sheba, come out!' She'd grabbed her as she'd tried to slink in unnoticed, then handed her back to Lucy.

'Sheba wants to come with you!' Lucy had smiled and held her tight.

'We wish!' Helen had sighed. If it had been up to her, she would've piled them all in – Cherie, Stella, Tabs, Snowy, Sheba. And of course, cute little Mac, who at that moment was nowhere to be seen.

'Say goodbye, girls!' David had instructed. He'd seen the tears welling up on all sides and knew that it was time for a quick getaway.

Everyone had sniffed back the tears and waved, except Sheba, who had miaowed very loudly and squirmed about in Lucy's arms.

And now here they were, shake-rattle-and-rolling

up the mountainside in their ancient car, being forced to think of Monday and – yuck, ugh – SCHOOL!

'C'mon, life's not that bad!' their dad coaxed. There'd been a stony silence from the back seat all the way down Doveton Fell.

' 'Tis!' Helen and Hannah retorted.

'What, even on a lovely sunny day like this?'

'It's gonna rain!' Hannah said glumly, though the clouds over the fell hadn't gathered and moved in as she'd predicted. In fact, the purple heather on the hillside was bathed in late afternoon sun, and the curlews soared across a blue sky.

David was beginning to regret his mention of Monday. 'Count your blessings,' he suggested as he turned the car up the lane leading to Home Farm.

Helen sat gloomily trying to count them. 'Such as?'

'Such as Speckle!'

The black and white Border collie stood at the gate to greet them. The white tip of his tail wagged until it looked as if it might fall off.

Helen and Hannah spotted him at the same time

and felt a warm glow creep over them.

'Such as Socks!' their dad went on.

The little tabby cat sat on the gate, awaiting their arrival. Striped brown and black, with a white face and white socks, he looked sleek, well-fed and very happy to see them.

Their dad slowed the car almost to a halt. A pretty, light grey pony trotted to the wall of the field beside the farmhouse. The little dappled horse poked his head out into the lane, shook his white mane and whinnied loudly.

'Such as Solo!' David reminded them as he got out to unfasten the farmyard gate.

'Hi, Solo!' Hannah and Helen leaped out of the car after him. They ran and patted their favourite pony.

'Such as Sugar and Spice, Lucy and Dandy, and assorted hens and chickens!' Their dad was suddenly surrounded by the twins' furry and feathered friends. The rabbits hopped madly up and down their wire-netting run. The two geese waddled and flapped. Fat brown hens sprinted on spindly legs, zigzagging this way and that across the flagged yard.

'How many blessings is that?' he asked cheerfully when he returned to the driver's seat and edged the car into the farmyard at a snail's pace.

The warm glow had spread and shaped broad smiles on the twins' faces. They waited until the car had finally stopped, and the rattles and wheezes had fallen silent before they stepped out.

'Loads!' Helen whispered, stooping to stroke Speckle. 'Hi, Speckle. It's good to be back!'

The dog wriggled and wagged. He shook his whole body, from his head to the tip of his tail, with total pleasure.

And here came Socks, stepping along the top of the gate, daintily placing his white feet into position, perfectly balanced. The tabby cat judged a distance, crouched, then leaped. He landed on the roof of the parked car, level with Hannah's grinning face. Then he came up close, rubbed himself against her cheek and purred.

'Hundreds!' Hannah agreed about the blessings. Never mind school, or the sad parting from Lucy. To tell the honest truth, she and Helen couldn't wish for a more perfect life!

* * *

'That car sounds as though it's on its last legs!' Mary Moore said with a sigh.

It was later that same evening, after Helen and Hannah had settled back in at Home Farm. Their dad had driven to Nesfield again, to collect their mum from the Curlew, and now the twins could hear her complaining about the wheezy old banger as she came in through the door.

'I've never heard so many thumps and bangs and squeaks out of a car engine.' Mary let her bag drop to the floor and hung up her jacket on a hook in the hallway.

'Shhh!' Hannah hissed at Helen from their hiding place behind the kitchen door. Hannah was wearing a frilly apron their mum had once bought at a jumble sale and stuck in the back of a drawer. And she was standing, pad and pencil at the ready, prepared to take orders.

'I *am* shhh-ing!' Helen mouthed back. She smirked at Hannah's flowery apron, then adjusted her own wonky chef's hat. 'Gerroff, Speckle!' she warned in a high, squeaky voice, as the dog tugged at the hem of her white chef's jacket; another jumble sale find which was at least six sizes too big.

'There's nothing wrong with that car!' Out in the hall, David stoutly defended the jalopy. Already included in the plan to surprise Mary, he cleared his throat and suggested that they go in to the kitchen for a cuppa.

Mary glanced up the stairs and into the living-room. 'Where are the girls?' she asked, sounding disappointed that they weren't around to greet her. 'Don't tell me. I suppose they're out on the fell, riding Solo!'

'Hmm.' The twins' dad hid a smile and steered Mary into the kitchen.

The table was set with the best plates and cups. There were green checked napkins, white candles, and pink carnations in a slender green glass vase.

'Surprise!' Helen and Hannah jumped out from behind the door.

'What would Madam like to drink?' Hannah asked in her poshest voice. 'We have ordinary tea, Earl Grey tea, lemon tea, and yucky herbal tea!'

Mary laughed. 'Yucky herbal tea, please, Miss!'

Helen shot her hands out of the ends of her too-long sleeves and reached up to adjust her hat. Then she stepped forward. 'May I suggest that Madame tries a petite slice of our 'ome-made gateau!' she trilled. 'We 'ave ze chocolate cake, ze chocolate cake, or – er – ze chocolate cake!'

'Better make that the chocolate cake!' Mary decided.

As the waitress and chef scooted off to fulfil the order, David offered Mary a seat at the head of the table. She sat down with a happy sigh, saying how nice it was to be waited on for a change.

'One herbal tea!' Hannah announced, arriving with tray containing a steaming teapot and a jug of hot water.

'Ees it, 'ow you say, yucky enough?' Helen asked, coming up behind with a wedge of gooey gateau on a china plate. The cake oozed chocolate and smelled heavenly.

'Am I glad you two are back!' Mary smiled, lifting a spoon and tucking in.

'Oh drat, zere goes ze phone!' Helen frowned. Just when the chef and the waitress were about to sit down to their own slab of cake.

'I'll get it!' David offered. He sauntered out into the hallway, wasn't gone long, and came back in with a worried frown.

'Piece of cake, Dad?' Hannah asked, her own mouth full of chocolate butter-icing.

'Hmm? Erm, no thanks, love.' Still frowning he began to hunt around for his keys. 'I have to go out for a little while.'

'Who was that on the phone?' Helen asked.

'Erm. Lucy Carlton. Anybody seen my car keys?'

Helen paused as she raised her laden fork to her mouth. 'Is Lucy OK?'

'Yes – well, no, not really. She was a bit upset as a matter of fact. I said I'd drive back over there to help her look.'

'Look for what?' Hannah spotted the keys on the windowsill and grabbed them. She slipped them in to her dad's hand.

Whenever he had too many things to think about, David's words came out muddled. 'Not what. Who. Oh, thanks, love. I'll need to buy petrol while I'm out. Money!' He tapped his back pocket. 'Got some. Keys?'

'You're holding them in your hand!' Hannah prompted.

Her dad chinked them in his palm. 'Oh good. Yes, that's what Lucy was upset about. She said she's looked everywhere, and there's no sign of him. It's as if he's vanished from the face of the earth!'

To Helen, this was beginning to sound serious. She laid down her spoon and unbuttoned her white jacket. Then she took off her hat. 'Who's vanished?'

'Yes, Dad, who?' Hannah stood up from the table her face serious, the apron hanging loose from her neck.

He pursed his lips, ran once more through the things he needed. 'Do you two want to come?' he asked the girls.

'Course!' Whatever . . . *who*ever was lost, the twins definitely wanted to help.

They quickly took off their outfits. The cake was forgotten, the surprise treat spoiled.

'David!' Mary too stood up. 'Before you dash off, please tell me what's going on!'

Already at the door, with Helen and Hannah to

either side, he gave her a puzzled glance. 'Sorry, love, didn't I say? That was Lucy on the phone. One of her kittens has gone missing.'

'Which one?' Hannah gasped, though in her heart she knew.

'Mac!' Helen murmured. It could only be him.

Mac the mischief-maker. Rough, tough, adventurous Mac.

'The little black one,' David confirmed. 'Lucy hasn't seen hide nor hair of him since we left. So come on, girls, it's the Moores to the rescue!'

They were out of the door before him, racing for the car, waiting impatiently as it spluttered and coughed into life.

Bang-scrape-rattle. It set off out of the farmyard, down the lane.

And all Helen and Hannah could think as they drove back through Hardstone Pass was, *Come home, Mac! Please come back!*

Three

'Don't worry. This kind of thing happens all the time. We always manage to find the missing cat in the end.' Helen put on a brave face for Lucy's sake.

She, Hannah and their dad had searched the garden at Stonelea. They'd looked among the rose bushes, in the branches of the apple trees and down by the trickling stream. No luck. Mac was nowhere to be seen.

'Yes!' Hannah chimed in with the same confident message. 'Remember Mitch? We never thought we'd track him down before Joanna Day came to collect him!'

That search, at the start of their summer's stay a Stonelea, had taken them into town in pursuit of the cheeky black-and-white kitten.

'But we did!' Helen reminded Lucy. 'So we're bound to find Mac pretty soon.'

The Cat Lady nodded slowly. 'I hope you're right.'

'He'll come home when he's hungry,' David predicted, looking out at the long shadows stretching across Lucy's lawn. Cats criss-crossed the grass, going about their cat business. Stella stalked an invisible prey at the base of a tree. Tabs headed for the last patch of sun, lay down and rolled onto his back, paws in the air.

Lucy walked stiffly up the garden path and gazed up at the pink sky in the west. 'The problem is, Mac's too adventurous for his own good. He's the kind of kitten whose boldness could get him into trouble.'

Helen pictured Mac wrestling with the tablecloth earlier that day; the way he tumbled and came back at it, clinging on for dear life. And he always had that look in his eyes; a bright perky gleam that said, 'What next? C'mon, set me another challenge before I get bored!'

'Maybe he went exploring,' Hannah suggested. 'Only he went too far and got lost. We'll have to wait for someone to find him and bring him back.'

'How will they know where he lives?' Helen asked. The more she stood in the darkening garden, the harder it was not to worry.

Hannah frowned. Mac was too young to be wearing a collar with a name tag on it. 'They won't know. But they'll realise he's lost . . .'

'. . . And bring him in to the cat sanctuary!' Helen nodded hard. 'Yes, that's right. They'll fetch him back here!'

'But what if he's out all night?' As David and Lucy quietly discussed the problem in the cottage porch, Hannah found it was her turn to grow alarmed over poor little Mac. He was so small and the world at night was so big and – well, dark!'

'Cats like the dark!' Helen insisted. She jumped as a large grey bird flapped its wings and flew clear of the tree that Stella had just climbed. Pulling herself together as the wood pigeon clattered away, she risked a glance at her sister. 'You worried, Hann?'

Hannah nodded. 'Are you?'

'Yep. But don't let Lucy see.'

'OK.'

Together they went to join the grown-ups.

'We'll have to leave it for tonight,' David told Lucy. 'If Mac hasn't shown up by tomorrow morning, give us another call.'

'Oh, I couldn't possibly trouble you. You've done more than enough already.' The Cat Lady did her best to smile. 'I'm probably being an old fuss-pot.' She paused, sighed, then confessed. 'Only, I have a feeling that all is not well. Call it a sixth sense. No, no, that's silly!'

'No, it's not,' Hannah said. She for one trusted Lucy's 'feeling'. 'Can you put your finger on it and give us a clearer idea?'

'For a start, Sheba's not been herself since Mac disappeared.' The old lady pointed up the garden to her favourite companion. The black cat sat at the gate, still as a statue, gazing out at the road. 'She's been there for hours. She even refused to come in for her supper. And it was boiled haddock; her favourite.'

'What else?' Helen asked.

'Well, it's unusual behaviour for a kitten to stray too far. Since Mac arrived at Stonelea and decided to adopt Sheba as his mother, I've got used to seeing him go wherever she goes.'

'That's true,' Hannah agreed. All the signs seemed to point to the fact that something bad had happened. 'Listen, Lucy, we won't wait for you to call us in the morning. We'll come back anyway and begin a proper search.'

'Unless Mac turns up out of the blue,' David put in. He turned to the twins. 'You'll be on your own, I'm afraid. I have a photography job booked in for tomorrow morning, and it's at a time that can't be changed.'

'That's OK, we'll come on our bikes,' Helen told him, as she, Hannah and their dad set off up the path. 'We'll bring Speckle. He's sure to be a big help.'

At the gate, Lucy stooped to pick up Sheba and take her indoors. 'Of course, I'll carry on searching the house and garden as best I can,' she told them. 'I only wish I was younger and fitter!'

'We'll do it!' Hannah insisted. She closed the gate behind them, then looked the old lady straight in the eye. 'We'll be here bright and early. And we will find Mac, we promise!'

Tomorrow would be Saturday. Then Sunday, then school. Helen and Hannah's weekend plans to buy new pens and felt-tips, to clear the rubbish out of the bottom of their schoolbags and to make new pencil cases out of bright purple fake-fur would all have to go on hold.

Finding Mac was much more important than sewing a silly old pencil case. Even grooming Solo and cleaning his tack would have to wait.

'What are you thinking?' David asked as he drove into a spectacular sunset.

They'd chugged to the top of Hardstone Pass just as the sun sank behind the ridge of distant mountains. The jagged horizon shone with a rim of gold, melting to bright orange, then dusky pink.

Hannah and Helen had sat in silence in the back of the car on the homeward journey. They'd felt the day draw to a close and had watched bats flit from old stone barns. They'd felt sad and worried, and not at all like talking.

'We're thinking about Mac,' Helen muttered.

'Dad, can't this car go any faster?'

The engine coughed like a tired old horse. Even now that they'd set off downhill, it still spluttered and puffed.

'No. What's the rush?'

'I was thinking, the sooner we get home, the sooner we can go to bed and get up in the morning. Then the quicker we can dash back and help Lucy find Mac.'

'That's if we can sleep!' Hannah sighed. She had the kind of knot in her stomach that might stop her curling up under the duvet and falling asleep.

'Well, sorry, girls.' David cocked his head to listen to the ropey engine. 'I can't squeeze any more speed out of her.'

Chug-chug-rattle-shake. The car made it down the hill to Doveton village.

'What's wrong with it?' Helen asked. She could hear a new rattle from under the bonnet and feel the whole car hesitate every time he put his foot on the accelerator.

'I haven't a clue!' he admitted. He ran a hand through his wavy brown hair, then took a good run at the last slope that would take them up the lane to Home Farm.

Rattle-chug-chug. Cough.

The car shuddered and slowed to a crawl.

'We'll have to get out and push it at this rate!' Hannah looked out at the dark hedges either side of the lane. Ahead she could see the lights from Fred Hunt's farm glimmering yellow through the dusk.

'Uh-oh!' David pushed the pedal hard against the floor. 'We're losing power!'

'Eject!' Helen cried. 'Emergency! Bale out before we start sliding back down the hill!'

'Stay where you are!' their dad ordered. 'This isn't a jet-fighter and you're not wearing a parachute!'

Chug-cough-chug-splutter-silence. There was a smell of hot metal and singed rubber hoses.

'We've broken down!' Hannah gasped.

'Brilliant, Einstein!' In spite of everything, Helen saw the funny side. They were stranded halfway up a mountain, in the dark, with steam coming out from under the bonnet.

'We've got a radiator leak!' Too late, David

spotted the fault. 'The engine's been overheating. That's why it's packed in!'

'Starship to Control! Priority message! Are you receiving us?' Helen giggled. 'We have a power failure in the booster rocket. We're drifting off-course and a stray asteroid is on collision course! Advise, please!'

'OK, everybody out.' Her dad gave up on the car and decided to finish the journey on foot.

'Do we have to?' Hannah protested.

'Yes. Unless you want to spend the night out here.'

'Abort!' Helen said in a metallic, robot-type voice. 'Control to starship; your orders are to abort the mission. Repeat; abort the mission!'

'Yeah, funny!' Hannah climbed out. 'Dad, we're blocking the lane. What're we gonna do about that?'

'Push!' he ordered. 'We'll leave the car in this gateway and explain to Fred on the way up. Tomorrow, I'll phone the garage and get them to tow it away.'

So they got behind the car and pushed it on to the grass, then left it steaming by the roadside.

Then they set off on the half-mile walk home.

'This is just what I don't need,' the twins' dad sighed as they trudged up the hill. They'd approached the lights of High Hartwell, knocked on the door and told Fred their problem. The farmer had offered them help with transport the following day, and David had gratefully accepted. Still, he was feeling low as they finally arrived home.

'There's one good thing,' Hannah said quietly to Helen. They stood in the yard and gave their dad time to go ahead and break the bad news to their mum.

Helen looked up at the crescent moon rising over the fell. 'What's that?'

'At least the problem with the car took our minds off Mac for a bit.'

Helen frowned. 'Did it?' If she was honest, all the messing about with the starship messages had been a big act. Below the surface, she was still really worried.

Hannah too stared up at the moon. 'No!' she admitted. Poor little Mac, lost and alone. Was he stuck up a tree? Had he wandered near a busy road? Was he hungry, thirsty, cold and afraid?

'I don't know about you, Hann,' Helen sighed. 'But tonight I don't think I'm gonna sleep a single, solitary wink!'

Four

'You two look terrible!' David told Hannah and Helen early next morning. He and Mary had been up since the crack of dawn, trying to organise life without a car.

'Thanks, Dad. You don't look too good yourself,' Hannah muttered.

His hair was sticking up, he had bristles on his chin and marmalade down the front of his T-shirt.

'Didn't you sleep?' Mary asked them, guessing the reason behind the bleary looks.

'Uh,' Helen grunted. She wondered how her mum always managed to look so fresh and sound so cheerful, even at half past seven in the morning.

'Here's our lift into Nesfield!' David warned. He'd glanced out of the window and spotted Fred Hunt's mud-covered Land Rover. 'Are you ready?' he asked Mary.

'Yes. Cool, calm and collected; that's me.' Giving the girls a quick kiss on the tops of their heads, she grabbed her bag, then made for the door. 'How about you, dear?' she asked him sweetly. 'Are you ready?'

'Present and correct!' The twins' dad clicked his heels together and stood to attention.

'Er, David . . .' Mary pointed to the marmalade stains. 'And, er . . .' This time it was his stubbly chin that came under scrutiny. 'You can't tell me you plan to turn up at a professional photo-journalism job looking like that?'

'Ye-es!' he protested. 'What's wrong with me?'

'Don't ask, Dad!' Helen advised, her mouth full of toast. She and Hannah planned a quick breakfast, then a speedy cycle ride across to Stonelea.

'Everything!' Hannah chimed in.

'Love you too, girls!' David retorted, giving his sticky chest a quick rub with his fingers. Then he picked up his camera bag from the table and rushed out.

A moment later he was back. 'Good luck!' he said breathlessly. 'I'll keep my fingers crossed for you and little Mac!'

'Me too,' Mary promised. 'And remember; don't do anything rash!'

'We won't!' the twins promised glibly.

Their mum hesitated at the door. 'Well, I mean it. *Don't!* No mad dashes across busy roads, no staying out if the weather turns bad, no unnecessary risks!'

They looked up at her through narrowed eyes. 'We won't!' Secretly they were thinking, *We'll do whatever it takes to get Mac safely home!*

'I thought for a sec that Mum was going to say we couldn't go!' Hannah gasped as she sped after Helen down the lane. Speckle was loping in the long grass at the roadside, easily keeping up with the two bikes.

'I don't see how she could stop us.' Helen put on the brakes as she spotted two riders approaching up the hill. 'Not after we'd promised Lucy!'

Hannah jammed on her own brakes, recognising their friend Laura on Sultan and their new neighbour, Polly Moone from Manor Farm, on Holly. The two girls rode quietly up to the twins, waiting for Hannah to take hold of Speckle's collar and keep him quiet.

'Hey, you two. We were coming to see if you wanted to ride with us.' Looking confident and healthy on her gorgeous chestnut thoroughbred, Laura greeted them with a broad smile.

'Sorry, can't!' Helen said hurriedly. A pity, but they didn't have any choice.

'Maybe tomorrow,' Hannah suggested.

'Can't tomorrow,' Polly put in. 'I have to get ready for – yuck – SCHOOL!' She rolled her eyes from under the brim of her hard riding hat.

'Ugh!' they all groaned at once, then shuddered.

'How about later today then?' Laura wanted to know.

The twins and Speckle squeezed past the horses in the narrow lane. 'Maybe!' Helen threw back over her shoulder as they pedalled on.

Then they had to slow down again as Fred Hunt's Land Rover approached. As it happened, they were able to pull in to the gateway where their broken-down car stood.

'Ah, girls!' The old farmer leaned out of his window. 'I've just dropped your mum and dad off in town! Mary asked me to pass on a message if I saw you before you went off to Stonelea!'

'Uh-oh!' Helen could feel an extra chore coming on. 'Couldn't you pretend you didn't see us?' she asked Fred.

He raised his bushy white eyebrows. 'Well, Hannah, I don't think that would be right . . .'

'She's Helen!' Hannah put in. 'No, Fred can't lie about seeing us,' she told Helen primly. 'We have to see what Mum wants.'

Ignoring Helen's scowl, Fred passed on the information. 'Your mum would like you to look in the car boot for your suitcases and take them back to the house before you set off to look for the kitten.'

'Ohhh!' Helen sighed, like a balloon with a hole in it. 'Why right now?'

Fred tried to keep a straight face. 'Because, little

Miss Soap-opera-queen, your mum says you're bound to have a stack of dirty washing and she wants you to put all the white things in the washing-machine, ready for hanging out on the line when she gets back from the Curlew. She says she should have reminded you about it yesterday, but you all had other things on your mind.'

Reluctantly Hannah accepted the order. 'C'mon, let's do it.' She noticed that Speckle had already picked up the gist of what was going on and run over to the car ahead of them.

'What if the boot's locked?' Helen pointed out.

About to drive on, Fred laughed and shook his head. 'Sorry; no such luck. Your dad says he left the boot open in all the confusion of the car breaking down – all you have to do is press the catch.'

So Hannah reached the gateway and ordered Speckle to sit. 'Stay down,' she told the collie. 'It's only dirty washing; nothing to get excited about.'

Speckle whined and stretched his sensitive nose towards the boot. His ears were laid flat, his nostrils flared as he sniffed anxiously from a safe distance.

'What's wrong with him?' Helen wondered. Forgetting her grumps, she laid down her bike and went to talk nicely to Speckle.

'You hold him,' Hannah advised. 'This catch is a bit stiff. I'm having a problem getting it open.'

'Hurry up!' Minutes were ticking by and Helen knew that Lucy would be wondering where they had got to.

'I am hurrying!' Hannah pressed her thumb hard against the metal button.

Click! It responded at last and released the boot lid.

'Phew, what a stink!' She turned up her nose as a foul smell wafted out of the dark space.

'Probably your old trainers!' Helen muttered.

'Hah!' Easing open the lid, Hannah reached inside for the nearest suitcase. Then she felt something sharp prick the back of her hand and quickly pulled it back.

'Ouch!' she gasped.

'Oh, here, let me!' Rushing to take over, Helen forgot about Speckle. She let go of him and watched crossly as he bounded forward towards the open boot.

'It smells like . . . like!' Hannah didn't want to say.

'Pooh!' Helen cried when she got a whiff.

Yes, poo! Like some kind of wild animal had wormed its way in to the boot and spent the night there.

Woof! Speckle barked and scrabbled at the back bumper.

'Down, boy!' Hannah tried to pull him away.

Meanwhile, Helen reached inside. She seized the handle of the nearest suitcase and began to tug.

'Ouch!' Something had scratched her too. When she looked, there was a long, thin, red line across her knuckles.

Woof! Woof! Speckle had completely lost control. His claws scratched at the paintwork as he tried to jump into the car.

Meee-aaaoww! A cry from the dark boot made Helen and Hannah jump a mile.

Their jaws dropped, their muddled brains worked slowly.

'Was that a . . . cat?' Hannah whispered.

Helen crept slowly forward once more.

Meee-aaa-owwwww!

She saw two bright green eyes, a set of shiny sharp white teeth. 'Yes!'

Wooo-ooof! Speckle clambered in.

Miaow! A black kitten shot out like an arrow.

'Mac!' they both cried.

Helen lunged to catch the kitten. Hannah fell sideways into the ditch. The lid fell down on Speckle, trapping him inside the boot. Silence, then a muffled woof!

'Come back!' Not knowing whether to chase Mac or rescue Speckle, Helen dithered.

'Quick, he's getting away!' Hannah scrambled out of the ditch in time to see Mac beat a hasty retreat up the lane.

'You run after him! I'll try to open this lid!' Helen hurt her thumb as she pressed the lock hard, but to no avail.

By this time, the small kitten had a fifty-metre lead. But Hannah set off like on Olympic sprinter. With luck, she would catch up with him before he reached High Hartwell's farmyard.

With luck!

Brilliant! Why did Fred have to choose that

moment to drive his big yellow tractor out into the lane.

'Watch out!' Hannah yelled at the farmer. Her hair flew back from her face, the wind billowed through her T-shirt as she raced after Mac.

Chug-chug. The tractor rumbled on.

'Fred, stop!' Hannah waved both arms, glad when he saw her and pulled on the brake.

The kitten swerved around the yellow metal monster and cut across the farmyard, scattering Fred's hens as he ran. He was heading for the barn, which was where Fred's wife, Hilda, milked her small herd of goats.

'Call Lucy Carlton!' Hannah yelled at the farmer as he stepped down from his high driving seat. Down the lane, she could hear a full-blooded bark from Speckle, which meant that Helen had opened the boot lid at last.

Fred looked puzzled. 'What's going on? Why should I call Lucy?'

'To tell her the good news; say we've found Mac!' Hannah pointed frantically towards the small black shape hurtling through the barn door. He was like a Tom and Jerry cartoon character, only he was the mouse. 'Well, not quite!' she admitted, moving in fast to close the wide door. 'When I say, "found", I mean he's somewhere in your barn!'

'Right, I'll tell her,' Fred promised, hurrying off towards the house as Helen and Speckle arrived on the scene.

Helen was huffing and puffing. 'After all that!' she gasped. 'Mac keeps us up half the night worrying about him, and all the time he's stowed away in the back of our car!'

Panting, leaning with her back against the flaking red door, Hannah nodded. 'Using our boot as a cosy hotel while we rack our brains to find him!' Typical Mac!

'What now?' Helen asked.

'Here's in here somewhere. I suppose we go in to take a look!'

Helen went right up to the door and peeped through a crack. 'It's dark in there . . . er, Hann!'

'What?' Hannah clenched her fists and prepared herself for the task of cornering the runaway.

Through the narrow gap, Helen could make out stacks of haybales, wooden stalls with a central aisle. She heard the clip-clop of hooves, the clatter of sharp horns against the partitions, the high narrow bleat of Hilda's goats.

She turned to confront Hannah with the latest problem. 'The barn's dark . . . and big . . . and, well . . . not exactly empty!'

Five

'Goats don't hurt you!' Hannah insisted. She opened the door of Fred's barn a tiny crack.

Thud! Two horns and a bony head crashed against the other side of the door, slamming it shut.

Hannah pulled her fingers away from the rim in the nick of time. 'Well, not on purpose!'

Tramp-tramp-clatter! Hilda's goats stampeded up and down the central aisle.

'If you think I'm going in there to find Mac, you're crazy!' Helen frowned. 'Goats have horns and hooves and a bad temper; especially when they have kids to look after. If we try to get past them, we're gonna get trampled to death!'

Hannah gazed up at the flaking door and worn stone walls of the Hunts' barn. Helen had a point. She knew that the nannies in Mrs Hunt's herd had given birth in May and that the mothers wouldn't take kindly to strangers entering their barn. 'So what're we gonna do?' she whispered.

'Maybe there's another way in.' Helen was thinking of a side door, well away from the rampaging goats.

'Yes, there is,' a quiet voice broke in. Mrs Hunt had picked up a garbled message from Fred and come outside in her slippers to see if she could help. She was a small, shy woman with a tight bun of white hair and dark eyes that took in everything without flapping. 'I hear a kitten has taken refuge in there, and I can tell that Nancy and the rest aren't too pleased about it.'

Bang-thump-thud! The nanny-goats' hooves warned the twins not to enter.

'Come this way!' Mrs Hunt nodded and smiled, then led Hannah and Helen down the side of the barn. She pointed to a flight of stone steps leading to a hayloft stuffed to the rafters with freshly baled, sweet-smelling hay.

'Oh, thanks!' Helen sighed with relief. The hayloft would give them a good vantage point to search the barn. They would be looking down on the goats from a safe position, able to sit tight and wait for Mac to show himself.

Hannah was first up the steps, closely followed by Speckle. He took them two at a time, pink tongue lolling, whining eagerly to be allowed to help.

'No, Speckle, come here!' Helen called from ground level. As Hannah reached the entrance to the loft, the dog's head and tail drooped in disappointment. 'Come down!' Helen insisted. 'You'll scare Mac away if you go in there. You'll have to wait for us down here!'

Slowly Speckle turned. Head hanging, he came down the steps.

'Good dog!' Hannah urged from above.

'I know, it's not fair!' Smiling, Mrs Hunt took hold of the Border collie's collar. 'You wanted to be the hero, and they won't let you. But you come inside the house and see what nice treat I can find . . .'

Hannah watched Speckle retreat with his tail

between his legs. 'C'mon!' she hissed at Helen. By this time, Mac could have found himself a really good hiding place inside the Hunts' cluttered, noisy barn.

She went ahead, clambering through the high entrance and picking her way between the bales of scratchy, tickly hay. She found that stray wisps caught in her hair and went down her T-shirt, and that the rising dust was likely to make her sneeze.

'Can you see anything?' Helen asked from behind.

'Yeah – hay! *Aaatchoo!*' Hannah tunnelled to the top of the stack and came level with the strong, rough beams that supported the roof of the barn. From here she could look right down into the central well. 'And goats!' she reported.

Helen emerged. 'Puh!' She spat a wisp of hay from her mouth and pulled a cobweb from her cheek. Up in the rafters, a nest of baby swallows chirped and cheeped for food. Down below, a dozen pale cream nanny-goats and their kids trotted restlessly to and fro. 'I feel dizzy!' she gasped, drawing back from the edge.

'Don't look down!' Hannah's eyes had got used

to the semi-dark and were starting to pick out more detail. She made out one of Fred's old tractors rusting in a corner of the barn, other pieces of farm machinery, and the stalls near the wide doors where Mrs Hunt milked her goats. And she noticed that the farmer's wife's favourite nanny had spotted them. Nancy was a big cream goat with bright yellow eyes and a clever look; the leader of the herd.

The old saying about looking for a needle in a haystack went round and round in Helen's head. This search for Lucy's black kitten felt a lot like that. 'We've got to think!' she told Hannah. 'We have to use our brains to work out where Mac would hide!'

Crouching at the edge of the loft, staring down at Nancy, Hannah agreed. 'OK. Mac will be hungry, won't he?' After a night locked in the boot of their car, there was no doubt about that. 'So he'll be looking for food.'

'What kind of food would he find in here?' Helen took up the train of thought.

Cheep-cheep-cheep! The baby swallows in the nest on the nearby rafter opened their wide yellow beaks. *Feed me! Feed me!* Worms, spiders, dragon-flies.

Hannah gasped and shot Helen a glance. 'That kind of food!'

Baby birds. Hannah nodded. Like it or not, that would be Mac's idea of a fine breakfast. *Yum-yum!*

'OK, this is the picture!' Helen said eagerly. As she spoke, she scanned the loft and the beams that ran across the width of the barn. 'Mac scoots in here, not realising it's full of funny animals with weird yellow eyes and sharp horns. Whoa! He doesn't like what he sees. He nips up on top of the old tractor and does his cat thing of climbing up in to the beams. Hey, he likes it better up here!'

'Yep!' Hannah was nodding so furiously that she lost her footing on the slippery bales and slid down a level. She pulled herself up and took over the story. 'So he stays up near the roof while we mess around outside. He hears the baby birds – there's probably more than one swallows' nest in a barn this size – and he settles down in a dark corner, listening, waiting . . .'

By now the image was so strong in Helen's mind that she thought she saw black kittens everwhere.

Each shadow was Mac crouching on a beam, hiding in a corner, burrowing into the hay. 'My eyes are playing tricks!' she complained, crawling as near to the edge as she dared.

Below them, Nancy had obviously had enough. No one came in to her barn without permission. She fixed the twins with an evil look, tilted back her head and began to complain.

The noise started as a high-pitched snicker. Then Nancy opened her mouth and let out a bray that filled the whole barn. The bray grew in volume, went on and on, rising to an ear-splitting bawl that shattered the peace of the whole fellside.

'Aagh!' Hannah sat back, her hands over her ears.

'I'm going deaf!' Helen muttered. 'Can't someone make her stop!'

'Look!' The din must have roused every living creature for miles around. Hannah pointed to two swallows flitting and swooping through the rafters, then hovering near their nest. The birds twittered and fussed amidst Nancy's tuneless racket, darted to drop titbits into their babies' mouths, then swooped away again.

'Ouch!' Helen still couldn't stand the noise. She stuck her fingers in her ears and backed away into the furthest corner of the loft.

And it seemed that something else was trying to escape the goat's deafening warning. There was a rustle in the hay, a tiny squeak from behind a bale, then the glint of light green eyes.

'Mac?' Helen whispered.

Or was this just another black shadow, a trick of the light?

Her fingers still in her ears, Helen crouched for a closer look.

Let me out! The creature in the corner crept under cover through the hay. A glimpse of black fur, a small paw, the tip of an ear . . .

'Hannnah!' Helen hissed. 'It's Mac! He's over here!'

Neeyaagh! Neeyaagh! Nancy bawled.

The kitten was desperate; he had to get out. He rustled through the hay, disappeared behind a bale, and came out again close to the exit.

'Catch him!' Helen saw that Hannah was closer.

Hannah raised herself, ready to pounce. She planned a rugby tackle before Mac had time to make it to the stone steps; pictured a soft landing in the hay, a happy ending for Lucy.

'Now!' Helen squeaked.

Hannah threw herself headlong across the bales. She clutched frantically . . . and came up with two handfuls of hay.

With a swift swerve, Mac was out of the door. He was down the steps, flashing across the Hunts' farmyard, out of the gate.

'Hello there, girls!' Fred was at the farmhouse door when Hannah and Helen scrabbled into view. He hadn't seen Mac's latest bid for freedom. He looked up at them with a broad grin. 'Lucy says to tell you thank you very much for cornering the kitten in our barn. She'll be up here to deal with him just as soon as she can find someone to give her a lift!'

'We spoke too soon!' Hannah wailed. She'd lost sight of Mac in the lane, but had a strong feeling that the kitten had headed up the hill towards Home Farm.

'Great! Well done!' Helen couldn't help blaming Hannah for missing her chance. 'At this rate, we'll never get to join Laura and Polly on that ride this afternoon!'

'Yeah, well what about you?' Hannah retorted, eyeballing her sister. 'You were this close to him in that corner! You could've reached out and grabbed him. So why didn't you?'

'Girls, girls!' Mrs Hunt emerged from the house with Speckle and soon saw what had happened. 'You've no time to waste arguing about whose fault it was. Not while the kitten is still on the run!'

'Right!' They both saw the sense of this. They would have to argue it out later.

'C'mon, Speckle!' Helen cried. 'Find Mac. Good boy, find the kitten!'

'Uh-huh, uh-huh, uh-huh!' All this running was bad for her, Hannah knew.

Up the lane after Speckle, into the yard at Home Farm. A quick sniff around the stone trough where their mum had planted geraniums, a scout around their own barn, then out again into the lane.

'Uh-hu, uh-huh! Are we sure Speckle knows what he's doing?' Helen caught Hannah up as she followed the dog over the stone stile into one of the fields belonging to Crackpot Farm.

'You got a better idea?' Hannah gasped.

Speckle streaked across the tussocky grass, between thistles, in amongst a golden carpet of buttercups. His lean black and white shape loped evenly and in a straight line round the back of the Lawsons' farm.

Helen caught her breath, then climbed the stile. 'You're right,' she admitted. When had Speckle ever let them down?

'How can a kitten be so hard to catch?' Hannah's throat was dry, her lungs aching.

'I don't know, but we'd better catch up with him before he reaches Sam's place, otherwise it's just mountains for miles and miles after that!' Helen didn't fancy turning the sprint into a marathon.

'Talking of Sam . . .' Hannah gasped.

A fair-haired boy of their own age appeared on a bike at the gate to Crackpot Farm. He didn't seem to see them, and carried on practising, raising the front wheel off the bumpy ground to balance for a few seconds on one wheel, then slamming the front of the bike back down.

He was too far away to call, and too busy rehearsing his trick. But then the twins saw Speckle make a sudden swerve through the buttercups and head for Sam. Helen and Hannah were able to make a short cut and almost catch up with the dog as he bounded up to the boy on the bike.

'Sam, Sam, did you see . . .'

'. . . A black kitten?' Helen finished Hannah's gabbled sentence.

Say yes! Hannah willed him.

'Yep,' Sam said casually, showing off on his bike.

'And I saw you and your dog chasing it after it had shot off from High Hartwell.'

'It's not an "it", it's a "he"!' Helen said crossly. Why did Sam have a smirk on his face? Didn't he ever take anything seriously? 'Which way did Mac go?'

Sam landed his bike with a thump, put on the brakes and squealed to a halt. 'He came right through this gate and across this yard.'

'And . . . ?' Hannah demanded. Sometimes she could throttle Sam Lawson. Why, for heaven's sake, hadn't he stepped in to help them corner Mac if he'd seen the chase?

He shrugged. 'Do you expect me to know everything?'

With one eye on Speckle, who sniffed around the doorstep into Sam's house, Helen allowed her hopes to rise. 'Did he go inside?'

Sam wheeled round and cycled fast out of the gate. 'Nope.'

'Is he still in the yard?' Hannah ran forward to look under Sam's rabbit hutch and behind the dustbins. Speckle was still busy tracing scents, but for the moment he seemed to have lost Mac's trail.

'Nope.'

This time, as Sam got ready to repeat his trick, Helen stepped firmly in front of him. 'Where, then?'

There was another squeal of brakes as he almost shot over his handlebars. 'D'you want me to break my neck?' he demanded.

Helen fixed him calmly with her dark brown eyes. She didn't care if Sam decided to be sulky with them all through next week and up till Chrismas if he felt like it. All she needed was one simple piece of information. 'No. I want you to tell us which way Mac went.'

'OK, if it'll get you two out of my hair.' There would be no peace until he told them, Sam knew.

So he turned his bike round and pointed up towards the rugged, rocky horizon. 'Your precious kitten went thataway,' he said with the same smirk and a half-laugh. 'It looks like he got it into his stupid head to go off and climb a mountain!'

Six

It was at a time like this that Hannah and Helen realised that Home Farm really did stand on the edge of wild, wild country. Forget cosy cottages with roses round the doorway. Think bleak, cold, grey fells and cutting winds. Think emptiness.

Beyond Crackpot, the mountains rose to rocky summits across a steep stretch of scrubby moorland. Fast running streams cut through the hillsides, falling over flat ledges of green slate, tumbling into deep, clear pools.

And nothing grew except heather and ferns, with one or two twisted hawthorn trees providing poor shelter for the long-haired, lonely sheep.

'How much further do you think we should go?' Hannah stopped for breath by a stile. She looked up at a slope of grey shale and loose boulders, and beyond that a narrow ridge which linked Doveton Fell with Rydal Fell. Way in the distance, High Peak had disappeared under a thin veil of white cloud.

Helen narrowed her eyes and wached Speckle head on across the loose shale. 'We keep going until we find Mac!' she said firmly. 'And Hann, before you say anything; I know what Mum told us . . .'

'Don't take risks!' Hannah reminded her anyway. If anyone asked her, she would have to admit that following Speckle up the steep, deserted mountain counted as a definite risk. 'What if one of us falls?' she asked.

'We won't!'

'But what if?'

Helen turned her back on Hannah and glanced down the valley at the toy-sized farmhouses and the silver strip of Doveton Lake glittering in the sun. She took her time to weigh up the situation.

'OK, this is getting a bit hairy,' she admitted.

Up this high, the wind blew hard and the temperature dropped. There was always the chance that the weather could suddenly turn, that the mist over High Peak could sweep across the summits and envelop them. 'But what choice do we have?'

Hannah sighed, then nodded. 'I know. If we turn back now, we've got no chance of tracking Mac down.'

'Right. And Lucy's relying on us.'

'I expect she's on her way to High Hartwell right this minute, after what Fred told her.'

'We can't let her down!' Helen insisted.

As they talked, Speckle covered the ground. He'd reached the ridge leading to Rydal Fell and chosen to follow a track used by walkers on this remote hillside.

'I suppose it looks a bit safer up there.' Hannah was glad to see that Mac's trail led along a proper path.

'Yeah, c'mon!' Helen made up her mind to go on. She climbed the stile and began to scramble over the loose, flat stones to join Speckle.

'Watch it!' Following behind, Hannah had to

jump clear of the small avalanche of jagged stones that Helen's feet had set in motion. Then she found that it was hard to make progress. For every step that she took forward, she slid back half a step.

'Try going down on all fours!' Helen suggested, taking a leaf out of Speckle's book. 'It's easier to balance!'

Hannah tried it. She felt like a toddler, crawling on hands and knees. 'I'm glad no one's watching!'

'Yeah, but it works!' Helen scrambled up to the winding track and set off quickly after the Border collie. In the distance, she could see a small knot of figures in bright red and orange jackets, all carrying rucksacks and heading their way.

Hannah arrived on the path and brushed dirt off her hands. 'We can ask these walkers if they've seen a black kitten!' she said, her hopes suddenly rising once more.

They strode eagerly towards the four hikers; two men and two women. The men walked in front. They carried maps in plastic envelopes slung round their necks, and wore patterned knitted hats, long woollen stockings and stout boots.

' 'Scuse me, have you seen . . . uh-huh, uh-huh –

a black cat?' Hannah asked, meeting the men at full gallop. She'd stopped them by a wooden post bearing a sign which gave directions. *Lake Rydal, 2 miles. Doveton Lake, 3 miles*.

The first man; Orange Anorak, sniffed and pointed crossly to a notice fixed to the name-post. *Keep to the paths*. 'Can't you read?' he barked.

'Erm . . .' Hannah backed off.

'We saw you, so don't deny it!' Red Anorak spoke harshly. 'You just climbed over the scree. Have you any idea what damage that does to the mountain?'

'Yes, sorry!' Hannah felt herself go red. 'But this is an emergency!'

'We could report you to the Ramblers' Association for this!' Orange Anorak refused to let them off. He looked like every nightmare teacher, crossing-patrol person and car park attendant rolled into one. 'That is precisely the sort of thing that gets fellwalkers a bad name!'

'And you should keep that dog on a lead.' Red Anorak was just as bad as Orange. He pointed at Speckle, who snuffled and sniffed around one of the women, as if picking up an interesting scent.

'Down, Speckle!' Helen warned. 'Sit!'

'Is he vicious?' Mrs Red Anorak shrank up against the signpost. 'Peter, get him away from me. You know I'm allergic to dogs!'

'He's not vicious,' Helen tried to explain as she caught hold of Speckle's collar. The dog had already sat quietly, cocked his head to one side, and looked up at her with a puzzled expression. He didn't understand why he couldn't get on with his job of tracking Mac.

'Not keeping to the paths. Failing to keep your dog on a lead.' Orange Anorak listed the twins' countryside crimes. He tut-tutted as though they were beyond help. 'I suppose next thing we know, you'll be forgetting to shut gates and throwing litter all over this beautiful fell.'

'No we won't!' Now Helen was getting mad. She and Hannah loved the mountain just as much as these Anoraks claimed they did. 'Look, have you seen a black kitten, or not?'

'Oh dear, I'm allergic to cats as well . . .' Mrs Red Anorak looked round in alarm, as if there were a dozen kittens hiding behind the rocks, all ganging together to make her skin come up in great red lumps.

It was the fourth member of the hiking party who finally spoke sense. 'Liz, calm down. Forget your allergies for a moment. And Geoff, Peter, give these poor girls a break.' The woman gave Helen and Hannah a sympathetic look. 'Let's see if I can help,' she offered. 'You're obviously in quite a state about this missing kitten.'

'He's called Mac!' Hannah jumped in with the information. 'He's only about four months old. He's black all over!'

'Hmm. Doesn't a black cat bring good luck?' As the other three members of her group grunted and shuffled to one side, the helpful woman listened thoughtfully. 'So what's a tiny little scrap of a thing like that doing up here?'

'He ran away!' Helen explained. 'Well, first of all he stowed away in our car. But the car broke down and we didn't know he was there. So he spent the whole night in the boot. Then he managed to escape, and we've been chasing him ever since!'

'So he's hungry?' the woman asked.

Hannah nodded. 'The thing is, he's too young

to know what he's doing. He's never been up a mountain before.'

'I see.' As the sun went behind a cloud, the woman zipped up her jacket. 'This certainly is an emergency. But I'm sorry, girls, I for one haven't seen your kitten.'

'Oh!' Hannah and Helen's faces fell.

'But we will look out for him from now on.' She got ready to follow her grumbling companions, who had already set off on their official, keep-strictly-to-the-path route into the next valley.

'Thanks.' Hannah squared her shoulders and nodded at Helen to let Speckle go. The dog quickly picked up a trail that led in the opposite direction.

'Yeah, thanks.' Helen said quietly. They'd just wasted five minutes and got told off into the bargain. And there didn't seem to be another soul on the path between here and the summit of Rydal Fell. So now it was up to them and Speckle alone.

'Take care.' The kind woman smiled and waved them on their way. 'I hope the black kitten lives up to his reputation for being lucky!'

They nodded and thanked her, then set off.

Still ahead lay one big, high mountain and one very small cat.

'How long is a mile?' Helen asked.

Speckle had paused at another wooden sign. One finger pointed down into Nesfield, the other identified for walkers the high ridge of Three Peaks Way.

'One thousand seven hundred and sixty steps,' Hannah replied. She'd counted every one. 'If you reckon that one step is a yard, it's the same number as yards to the mile.'

'That's pretty big steps.'

'Yeah but we are running, so we're taking long strides.' Both Hannah and Helen wanted to convince themselves that they'd covered a lot of ground since they'd split off from the grumpy hikers. It surely meant that sooner rather than later, Mac's little legs would get tired and he would stop for a rest.

'Speckle wants us to take the high road.' Hannah pointed out that the dog had chosen his route and was forging ahead.

'Oh no; more steep drops!' Helen's voice

quavered. She didn't like it when the narrow track fell away sharply to either side. In fact, she didn't like heights, full stop.

'You'll be OK. Hang on to my T-shirt if you start to feel weird.' Hannah knew that this was no time for Helen to go dizzy on her. Luckily, she saw something that would take her sister's mind off the problem. 'Here come Laura and Polly!'

The twins saw the two girls making their way on horseback along the bridlepath that led up from the town. It seemed they'd taken the low route for their ride and were now planning to circle back

towards Doveton using the high track.

Laura's Sultan led the way, looking strong and confident. His chestnut coat shone, his dark mane had been plaited in a fancy style, and every piece of tack gleamed.

'Hey, you two; I thought you said you were busy!' Laura greeted them with a reproach. 'If you didn't want to ride with us, all you had to do was say it straight out.'

'We did! We do!' Hannah said hastily. 'We're not just messing about up here, pleasing ourselves.'

'What are you doing then?' Polly asked suspiciously. She reined Holly to a halt and waited for the answer.

'Don't ask!' Helen had just made the mistake of glancing right down into the valley. She felt her knees knock and her heart miss a beat.

'You're looking for something,' Laura guessed. 'Don't tell me – one of Mrs Hunt's nanny-goats has gone walkabout?'

'Close, but not quite.' It wouldn't have been so bad, Hannah thought, if Mac had been a goat. Goats belonged on mountains, whereas kittens didn't.

'One of John Fox's lambs?' Laura guessed again, scanning the high ridge.

'No. Kitten. Lucy Carlton's.' Hannah got the message across as fast as she could. Time was passing, Speckle was already two hundred metres along the ridge. 'Black. Called Mac. Seen him?'

'A cat? No way!' Polly cut in, letting them know they must be mad even to attempt to trace the kitten. 'Have you seen those clouds over High Peak? Don't you know what's going to happen to the weather if they blow this way?'

'Yeah, yeah!' Helen concentrated on looking up instead of down. She let Polly and Laura know that a spot of rain wouldn't throw her and Hannah off Mac's trail.

Woof! From the vantage point of a tall rock by the side of the track, Speckle let the twins know that he was on to something fresh.

'C'mon!' Hannah urged.

'Helen, are you sure you feel OK?' Laura was staring down at her from the comfort and safety of Sultan's saddle.

'Yeah – thanks!' If she kept her chin tilted up

and didn't let her gaze wander, Helen felt she could cope.

'I said, c'mon!' Hannah ran nimbly along Three Peaks Way, feeling the wind blow hard against her, hearing the sound of her voice torn from her mouth and flung skywards before it reached Helen still lingering by the signpost.

Laura stared even harder. 'Helen, you've gone a really funny colour.'

'No, I'm fine . . . honest!' She gulped and took a tottering step after Hannah.

'Kind of a mixture between green and yellow.' Polly didn't pull her punches as she described the way Helen looked. 'Are you sure you're not going to be sick?'

Helen's eyes flashed. 'I said I was fine!'

'So why are you gritting your teeth? How come you're you wobbling all over the place?'

Wobble-wobble-gulp. 'I'm not, Pol!' *Don't look down!*

'We'll keep an eye open for Mac on our way back!' Laura promised, her voice fading on the wind.

Don't look down! Helen clenched her jaw and

squeezed her eyes almost shut. Flashes of sunlight squeezed through the narrow gap and strange patterns floated across her vision. Her stomach seemed to have turned the wrong way up. She had to remind herself to breathe.

'Helen?' Fifty metres ahead, Hannah turned to wait.

'Yeah, coming! You go ahead!' That's what she thought she said, but she couldn't be sure as the whole world seemed to tilt and go in to a spin.

There was a sheer drop to her left. And Helen knew for certain that she was going to fall.

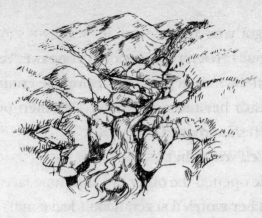

Seven

'Helen, it's me; Hannah! What on earth's the matter?'

She was falling . . . falling. There was nothing to cling on to. This was it; the end.

'Hen, open your eyes!' Hannah took her by the shoulders and shook her hard.

'I c-c-can't!' *What happened?* thought Helen. *Had Hannah fallen with her? Were they both tumbling through thin air, plunging to their deaths?*

'Yes you can. Open them!' Hannah pleaded. She took in Helen's sickly white face and rigid body. 'You're feeling dizzy, that's all. But

I've got you. You're safe.'

Slowly Helen risked opening one eye. Yep; that was the windswept sky up above, the ground firm beneath her feet. 'I thought I'd fallen over the edge!' she croaked.

'Well you didn't.'

She opened the other eye and came face to face with her worried sister. 'Don't leave me!'

'I won't. But you've got to get it together. Tell yourself that everything's OK.' Hannah didn't really understand this terror of heights, until she remembered herself and ghosts. At times, if she thought a place was haunted, her whole body could tremble and go into a cold sweat. Fear would hold her in its icy grip and it would be no good anyone telling her to be sensible; that there was no such thing as ghosts.

'I'm s-s-scared, Hann!' Helen felt her stomach lurch as she again caught sight of the way the path suddenly dropped away. 'I don't think I can move!'

'OK, shut your eyes again. Take a deep breath.' Hannah realised that it was up to her to get them out of this. 'Right, keep them shut and grab hold of the back of my T-shirt!'

Terrified, Helen fumbled to do as she was told.

'Think of something else. What would you most like to be doing right now?'

'Riding Solo.' The answer came into her head in an instant.

'Good. OK, you're riding him along the shore of the lake. There are boats on the water. Solo wants to trot but you're telling him to walk.' As she painted the scene, Hannah began to inch her way along the ridge. She felt Helen's grip on her T-shirt tighten, but at least she was holding on and managing to follow.

'Good boy, Solo!' Helen murmured in a faraway voice. 'Nice and easy boy; that's it!'

'Well done!' Now that she'd got her moving, Hannah hoped that Helen would start to relax. And once she'd steered her past this narrow bit to a flatter ledge up ahead, they would be able to take a breather and give Helen time to pull herself together. 'Just a bit further!' she promised.

'OK, Solo, now you can trot!' Her eyes still tight shut, Helen clicked her tongue. She strode more confidently, keeping hold of Hannah's T-shirt and allowing herself to be led. All the time, she kept firmly in mind the picture of herself riding their lovely grey pony by the calm, sunny lake.

'OK, lean against this rock.' Eventually, Hannah reached firmer ground. She guided Helen safely away from the dangerous side of the path, then made her open her eyes. 'Take your time,' she insisted.

Helen opened them a crack. The feel of the solid rock against her back was good. There was the root of an overhanging hawthorn tree to hang on to, and Hannah standing between her and the terrifying drop.

'Better?'

'A bit.'

'What do you want to do, Hen? Should we go on or turn back?' Though they'd made it this far, Hannah wasn't sure that her sister was fit to continue.

OK, so this next stretch looked pretty flat and un-scary, but who knew what was round the next corner? Besides, it turned out that Polly Moone had been right about the clouds sweeping down from High Peak. Helen could see them now, pulled by the wind down the side of the big fell, into the valley and pushed up again towards the slope where they stood.

'We should carry on!' She said in a determined voice. 'After all, we've made it this far.'

'But what if you turn dizzy all over again?' Hannah felt the first fine drops of rain carried in the wind.

'No, I'm over it!' (*Don't look down! Take deep breaths*.) 'Hann, if one little kitten can make it this far, then so can I!'

'You sure?' She pictured Mac up here in the wind and rain. The poor thing must be tired and frightened by now, and desperately wishing he'd never set off on this unlucky adventure.

Helen let go of the tree root and steeled herself to lead the way. (*Don't look down!*) She ignored the cold splashes of rain on her face and fixed her gaze on Speckle up ahead.

The dog had waited patiently for Helen to get over her fear of heights. He sat on the track for a few moments, watching her step boldly towards him, then trotted willingly to meet her. He wagged his tail and yapped, as if to tell her, *Well done, but could you please cut it out and follow me more speedily in future?*

'Yeah, yeah, Speckle, I hear you!' Helen laughed faintly. Wow, the wind was cold, and this rain was really coming down fast!

'Go ahead, find Mac!' Hannah urged the impatient dog, glad that he at least seemed to know what he was doing. 'I don't know what we'd do without you!' she whispered.

'Look, he's definitely telling us to follow him off the track!' Helen stopped to watch Speckle take a fork to the right. He disappeared into a tangle of ferns, the white tip of his tail bobbing up the steep hill.

Hannah frowned. 'The Anoraks wouldn't like that!' she muttered.

'Yeah, but a kitten can't read a notice telling him to keep to the track!' Helen pointed out. 'What are we supposed to do?'

'Follow Speckle,' Hannah agreed.

So they struck out after him, brushing aside the curling fronds of green fern to find a barely noticeable sheep track up the fell.

(*Don't look down!*) Helen pushed ahead,

feeling the wet ferns soak the legs of her jeans. Whenever she caught a glimpse of Speckle, he seemed to be extra eager; nose to the ground, sniffing excitedly and hardly aware that the twins were lagging behind again.

'Where did Speckle go?' Hannah caught up with Helen and peered anxiously up the slope. She shivered in the wind and rain, realising that she could no longer see very far ahead. The peaks of the fells had already disappeared in the downpour and clouds were rolling in around them as they stood.

'Over that next ridge.' Helen had seen the tip of his tail bob and disappear. She scrambled after him, hardly remembering to be afraid of the height in her anxiety to keep the dog within sight.

But that was going up. When it came to reaching the ridge and looking down into the next dip, it was a different matter!

'Ohhh!' Helen saw the deadly drop. Every bone in her body seemed to melt.

Hannah saw it too; a sudden, gut-wrenching, almost sheer cliff. The wind buffeted them and threw them off balance, driving the rain into their faces and chilling them through. 'No way!' she murmured.

If Mac really had chosen this route, it looked like an impossible one for them to follow.

Get a grip! Helen told herself. *Think of Solo and calm waters!* 'There must be more than one way down!' she hissed at Hannah. 'Yes, look; down by the side of that stream! That's where Speckle's telling us to go!'

So they edged along the dangerous ridge to a place where a narrow stream cut down the mountain into the next valley, finding its route between sharp rocks, through deep, black gulleys and splashing noisily over flat ledges.

'Good boy!' Helen gasped at Speckle as she joined him at the water's edge. She fought to control her nerves and to concentrate on the job of finding Mac. 'Where next?'

The dog barked and led them a few metres downstream. He ducked his head and yapped at them to follow.

'This is a dead end!' Hannah exclaimed, unable to hide her disappointment. She peered over the ledge where the dog was waiting, then back up at a jumble of giant, moss-covered boulders. 'Speckle, why did you bring us down here?'

He barked again; a short, sharp burst of sound against the background of rushing water. Then he jumped up at Hannah as if trying to convince her that he hadn't made a mistake.

Hannah sighed and shook a shower of raindrops from her fringe. She let go of the last few shreds of hope that they were about to find the kitten and stared up bitterly at the cascading stream. 'Let's go,' she said at last.

But Helen was thinking hard. 'Hang on a sec. This might seem like a dead end to us,' she pointed out, 'but cats can climb, remember. Suppose Mac made it this far. Speckle seems sure that he did. But then it gets cloudy and starts to rain. And cats don't like to get wet. So Mac is up against two different kinds of water; the pouring rain and this foaming, tumbling white thing called a stream.

Helen paused for breath, then rushed on. 'Suddenly climbing a mountain doesn't seem like fun any more. So what does he do?'

'He hides?' Hannah suggested.

'Exactly!' Helen pointed to Speckle nosing

about amongst the wet undergrowth. 'He finds the driest place he can and he hides there until the rain stops!'

'You mean, Mac must still be round here somewhere?' Hannah could see the sense in what Helen had said.

'Yeah, and it's not so much what *I* think!' Helen began to poke about under the ferns by the stream. 'This is where Speckle brought us. And when did you ever know him to be wrong?'

'True!' Hannah set to with new energy. She felt sorry that she had ever doubted their clever Border collie. And now she decided to stick by his side, searching for Mac wherever the dog went, certain that his sensitive nose and ears held the key to the lost kitten's hiding place.

'Don't you wish you could hear as well as a dog?' Helen hissed, thrusting aside the fern fronds and peering underneath. Her own ears were full of the splash of water against rocks.

Hannah was too busy following Speckle to answer. She struggled up a slippery boulder after him and crouched on a ledge above Helen's head. She and the dog were surrounded by smooth,

sheer rocks that would be impossible even for a cat to climb. She recognised that now they really did seem to have hit a dead end. So she leaned over the edge of the ledge and called down to Helen. 'Can you see anything?'

'Not a thing!' Helen called back. Not so much as a frog or even a worm moved in this thick, wet jungle.

Hannah rested back on her haunches and rubbed the raindrops from the tip of her nose. Speckle sat beside her, ears cocked, waiting expectantly.

'What?' she asked him.

His brown eyes stared questioningly look at her.

'What do you want?' Hannah insisted.

Yip! Speckle stood up and inched under the overhang above their heads.

'Yes, I know we're getting wet!' Hannah thought this was no time for him to play the wimp and seek the shelter of the overhang. She crawled into the dark, damp space, intending to persuade him back out.

Yip-yip!

Then, *Mew-mew-mew!*

Hannah stopped dead.

Mew-mew! The cry came from the depths of the cave. It was muffled and frightened; one of the most pathetic sounds Hannah had ever heard.

'Mac?' she whispered. Did she dare to believe it?

Yip! At last! Now do you get it? Speckle darted out of the way so that Hannah could see a pair of gleaming eyes.

'Oh, Mac!' Hannah sighed.

Lucy's kitten cowered under the overhang. His eyes were tiny points of green light in the black cave. And his thin cry when he saw Hannah said, *I've had enough of this horrid, rainy mountain. I'm tired and hungry. So if it's not too much to ask, could you kindly pick me up and take me home!*

Eight

'OK, this is the end of the adventure!' Hannah told Mac. She felt relief flood through her as she picked him up and crept back towards the edge of the slippery ledge.

The kitten cosied up against her; a small bundle of shivering fur.

'Helen, look who I found!' Hannah cried.

Helen looked up through the pouring rain. 'Thank heavens!'

'And thank Speckle!' Hannah watched the dog make his way down from the ledge. For a moment she wondered how she was going to follow him down the wet and difficult slope. The crashing waterfall to one side deafened her and she spotted awkward boulders which she would have to negotiate.

'Careful you don't drop him!' Helen called. She could see Mac squirming in Hannah's arms.

'Yeah, you try climbing down from here!' It was harder than Speckle had made it look when you only had two feet and your hands were full.

'Well, take your time!' Helen held her breath as she watched Hannah teeter on the edge of the rock. She greeted Speckle with pats and a great hug to tell him how clever he'd been to find little Mac.

'The problem is, this rock's slippy!' Hannah had tried the route that the dog had taken, but found she couldn't keep her footing.

'How's Mac?' Helen shouted up.

'Cold and wet. But I think he's OK!'

'If you climb halfway down, I can probably come up to meet you!' Rainwater trickled down the back of Helen's T-shirt as she craned her neck to see what Hannah was up to.

'No, stay where you are. I don't want you going all wobbly again!' Hannah tried another route, closer still to the tumbling water. She felt Mac cower close against her chest as cold, heavy splashes drenched them both.

She made it safely down to the midway point, conscious that Speckle and Helen were still staring anxiously up at them. By now her heart was beating fast and her muscles were tight with fear. One slip sideways, and she knew she and Mac could be dragged into the stream.

'Careful!' Helen too realised the danger.

'Never say an adventure's over till it's over!' Hannah muttered to herself. She looked back up at the overhang, then down the three metre drop between her and Helen, wondering how she'd suddenly got into this mess. 'OK, I'm gonna try heading for that flat rock!' she yelled.

Helen squeezed her eyes tight shut. 'I can't bear to look!'

Hannah planted one foot on a rock she thought she could trust. She shifted her weight forwards.

'Watch out!' Helen opened her eyes in time to see the chosen rock tilt with Hannah and Mac balanced precariously on it.

Too late! Hannah swayed first one way, then

another. The rock scraped loose from the boulder it was wedged against and began to slide back towards the waterfall.

'Jump!' Helen cried.

Hannah held on to Mac and jumped. She landed on the smooth, steep boulder, skidded and slid. The slope flung them sideways and sent them toppling headfirst, crashing into a sharp finger of rock which cut short their fall.

Silence. Helen had seen Hannah and Mac slide headfirst out of sight. For a split second she pictured them crashing over the edge of a sheer cliff into empty space. Her worst nightmare. She screamed at the top of her voice; 'Hannah!'

'Here!' The fall had knocked the breath out of Hannah. Her ribs ached and her leg seemed to hurt. But she was alive. And she still had hold of the kitten.

'Where? I can't see you?' Helen set off in the direction of Hannah's faint voice. She scrambled over the rocks, catching hold of ferns and finding handholds to pull herself up. Not once did she glance down and feel herself seized by terror. No; not now that Hannah was in trouble and she was the only one who could help!

Letting Speckle show her the way, she climbed until she reached a pointed rock. She found Hannah crumpled against it, her leg bent awkwardly beneath her.

Hannah felt Speckle's warm tongue licking her cheek. She groaned and turned her head to see Helen bending over her.

'Can you get up?' Helen whispered, trying to shield Hannah from the pouring rain.

Hannah tried, then shook her head. 'It's my leg!'

'OK, don't try any more. Just lie still.' Thoughts flashed through Helen's mind. Was the leg broken, she wondered. Could the injury be even worse? What if Hannah had broken her ribs, her back even . . . ?

First aid! What was it they said? Don't try to move anyone who's had a fall. You could make an injury much worse by disturbing them. A broken rib could puncture a lung. If the spine was broken, any movement could paralyse them for the rest of their lives!

Winded, bruised and battered, Hannah lay against the rock and groaned. Her teeth chattered with cold and shock. 'How's Mac?' she whispered.

Helen could only just see the kitten peeping out from the crook of Hannah's arm. He mewed loudly, opening his pink mouth and letting out an angry cry. 'He's fine! Hann, what're we gonna do now?'

'Wait. I'll be OK. Just give me a few minutes.' Once more Hannah tried to ease herself into a sitting position, but a pain in her chest made her flop back.

'No way.' Helen clenched her fists and came to a decision. 'You're not to move, OK? You stay exactly where you are and I'll go to fetch help!'

Weakly Hannah sighed, then nodded. 'Take Mac with you,' she pleaded.

Helen thought this was a good idea. If she took the kitten, then this was one thing Hannah wouldn't have to worry about. 'But Speckle stays here!' she said firmly. 'He can stand guard and look after you. If any walker comes by, he'll be able to bark and attract their attention.'

Knowing that they were talking about him, Speckle gave a quiet bark and settled himself down beside Hannah.

'How will you find your way back along the ridge without him?' Hannah wanted to know. Part of her longed for the dog to stay with her, but part of her knew full well that he could be useful to Helen if he went with her to find help.

'Speckle stays!' Helen repeated her decision, reaching to take Mac from his safe shelter in the crook of Hannah's arm. 'Listen, Hann, I'll be quick as I can. If I had a jacket to put over you to keep you warm, that would be better. But I haven't. So Speckle will have to lie up against you.' Gently she edged him towards the curled figure. 'Stay!' she insisted, standing up with Mac and picking out the best way back onto the ridge.

The dog rested his head against Hannah's arm and laid the length of his warm body against her.

'OK?' Helen checked one last time.

Hannah smiled weakly and shook her head. 'I'm scared stiff as a matter of fact!'

Helen glanced up at the bleak, rain-sodden ridge. 'Me too,' she admitted. 'But here goes!'

Scared or not, she had to do this.

Forget about her fear of heights. Concentrate on getting on to Three Peaks Way and fetching help.

Helen stumbled up the side of the stream, back the way they'd come. The rain came down hard and fast, the cloud clung to the mountain and blasted by in great grey swirls, so thick she could hardly see the rocks ahead.

It was only when the ground flattened out and she felt the renewed force of the wind that Helen knew she was back on the hikers' trail. It meant she must turn away from the wind and tread carefully along the worn track, taking care not to stray to right or left.

Clutching Mac close to her, she felt her way.

To the left was the sheer, deadly drop. She couldn't see it, but she could sense it. The mere thought took her breath away and made her heart knock against her ribs.

'This is all your fault, Mac!' she muttered grimly.

The kitten mewed unhappily, his face turned in towards her, his small body trembling.

The wind and rain buffeted them, the mist swallowed them, disguising every landmark and deadening all sound.

One hundred and fifty two, one hundred and fifty three ... Helen counted every doddering step. Sometimes she stumbled and almost fell, but somehow she always managed to keep her balance. Two hundred and twenty ... two hundred and eighty-four; one step was a yard. Surely soon she must come off the terrifying ridge.

But even then; even after she'd reached the signpost which pointed down to Nesfield and civilisation, there was a whole extra mile and a half to the town. And time was ticking by while poor Hannah lay injured by the stream. To her each second would feel like ten. Time would stretch out endlessly; she would grow afraid that Helen had fallen or got lost . . .

Looking up at the looming signpost, Helen double-checked the way to Nesfield. She made out the letters carved into the wood, hitched Mac more firmly under her arm and set off on the downwards path.

And still the rain drummed onto the ground and the mist swirled. A small dot in the middle of nowhere, Helen pushed on with only one thought in mind.

Then a new kind of drumming entered her head; deeper, more rhythmical than the rain. It came from high on the hill, from the direction of Doveton Fell, and as it drew near it began to sound to Helen's confused senses like horses' hooves pounding the earth.

She stopped and listened. Surely not.

Closer and closer; horses galloping, hazy grey shapes appearing through the mist. Two riders bent low over their horses' necks. Magnificent horses coming at full stretch along Three Peaks Way. Their hooves splashed through streams and thudded against the rocky ground.

Helen turned and ran towards them. 'Help!' she called. 'We're in trouble! Please stop!'

Nine

'Hannah?' Laura Saunders reined Sultan to a halt and peered at the shadowy figure running towards them through the mist.

'No, it's me; Helen!' Her heart beat so fast it practically jumped out of her ribcage.

Polly Moone came up up behind Laura and quickly jumped down from Holly's saddle. 'What's happened? Where's Hannah?'

'Oh, thank you!' Beside herself with relief, Helen couldn't give straight answers. 'We need help. We need Sultan and Holly to rescue Hannah. That is, if she can move. But maybe she won't be able to. Then one of you will have to ride and fetch an ambulance. In fact, Polly, you could do that right now. Laura and I will head straight back to Hannah!'

'Slow down, Helen!' Laura caught hold of her arm, almost pulling Mac out of his safe position. 'You found him!'

Helen nodded. 'Hannah did. Then she fell. She's hurt. Quick, Laura, we have to go back for her!'

'We knew something like this might happen!' Polly explained why she and Laura had decided to turn round and come looking for the twins. 'As soon as it started to rain, we thought we'd best head back to take a look!'

Standing in the rain, their sides heaving, Sultan and Holly gasped air into their lungs after their hard gallop.

'Will you ride into Nesfield and find a doctor?' Helen urged. 'Or an ambulance. Or Mountain Rescue. Anything! But do it quick!'

Nodding, Polly remounted. 'Where do I tell the emergency services to come?'

'On to Three Peaks Way, to the waterfall on the ridge that links Doveton and Rydal Fells. We'll keep a look out!' By this time, Helen was scrambling onto Sultan's back, tucking herself in behind Laura. She held Mac tight with one hand and slid the other round her friend's waist.

'Ready?' Laura asked.

Helen drew a deep breath. 'Yep.' For the third time that day, she got ready to face her worst fear.

But this time, Sultan's steady pace along the deadly ridge kept her calm.

'Easy!' she told herself, her face pressed into Laura's wet jacket. 'Nothing to it!'

When they heard the stream up ahead, Laura slowed down, then stopped. 'Is this the place?'

Helen could make out certain rocks more clearly than before and felt that the cloud might be lifting at last. 'Yes. We'd better tie Sultan up and head down on foot. It's too steep for him to try.'

'OK. Pop Mac into my saddlebag. We'll leave him here with Sultan, where he can keep warm and dry until we get back with Hannah.' Calmly Laura thought through what to do.

'It's fine,' she said, unstrapping a spare waterproof jacket as Mac wriggled and mewed not to be left in the dark canvas bag. 'He'll soon settle down, and there's no way he can escape if we buckle the flap tight.'

'Stay there!' Helen insisted as the little black face peeped out of the bag. Mac's front paws scrambled free until she gently eased him down out of sight and closed the flap.

Mew-mew! he cried. *It's dark in here! Mew!*

Hardening their hearts to his call, Laura led her horse to a sturdy hawthorn bush and proceeded to tie him up. Then, carrying the waterproof, she followed Helen over the edge, down the steep slope to where Hannah lay injured.

'Hann?' Helen whispered as they approached. She needed an answer to convince herself that Hannah hadn't fallen unconscious.

It was Speckle who heard her first. He picked up the sound of Helen's voice above the crash of the waterfall and barked loudly, guiding them to the right spot.

'Careful!' Helen warned, as Laura almost slipped on the mossy surface. Still no answer from Hannah, she realised. So she called her name a second time.

'Here!' Hannah replied.

Helen heard and let herself sag forward for a second. She breathed out hard, then continued on her way until she reached the unusual pointed rock that had broken Hannah's fall.

'I know, I know!' Hannah read the look on Helen's face. 'You told me not to move in case I'd broken something!'

Helen stared at her in surprise. Hannah was sitting with her back to the rock, legs straight out in front. Though her face was pale, she was obviously OK.

'I tried to stay still,' Hannah went on. 'But when I got my breath back, I found the fall had only winded me. My back's perfectly OK; see!'

'Hmm.' Helen frowned and tried to look stern, as Laura clambered down to join her. 'Are you sure?'

'Certain. But . . .' Hannah made a helpless gesture towards her left leg, 'this isn't!'

'Which bit?' Laura moved in quickly and quietly. She wrapped the spare jacket round Hannah's shoulders, then moved down to study the injured leg.

'My ankle!' Hannah winced as she tried to move

it. 'It's swollen up to twice its normal size and it hurts like mad!'

Laura frowned. 'It could be broken, I guess. Or else just badly sprained. They'll have to X-ray it at the hospital.'

'That's if I ever manage to get out of here!' Hannah sighed and looked up at the ridge. 'Trust me to fall down and cause a big problem!'

'You were only saving Mac's life!' Helen reminded her, then she explained that the kitten was warm and dry – and secure – in Laura's saddlebag. She held up her crossed fingers and grinned. 'We hope!'

'At least the rain's easing.' Laura looked up at the sky, wondering whether to risk trying to move Hannah on to the ridge. 'I think we'd better wait for the experts,' she decided.

'What's that noise?' Helen asked.

Speckle too had cocked one ear and was listening hard to the *chug-chug* churning sound coming from the clouds.

It was a deep, throaty sound; some kind of engine in the sky. Not a plane. More like a helicopter.

Then a shape swayed into view over the ridge. It was fat-bellied and long-tailed, with blades whirring.

'Tell me I'm seeing things!' Hannah groaned. 'This can't be real!'

Speckle stood up and barked at the giant machine.

'Mountain Rescue!' Laura exclaimed. 'Wow; Polly really did get things moving!'

The helicopter circled the ridge, tilted and flew in their direction. The pilot stared down from his clear cabin, spotted the girls and hovered overhead.

'But I don't need . . . !' Hannah felt her chilled body glow with embarrassment. Helicopters only came to the rescue when people were almost dead and had to be rushed to hospital. To prove that she didn't deserve all this fuss, she tried to struggle to her feet. 'Ouch!' she yelped, then collapsed back on to the ground.

'Yes, you do!' Laura insisted, watching the pilot's helper lower a rope with a cradle attached. 'If we don't use a helicopter, how else are we going to get you off this mountain?'

* * *

'It was *mega-mega*-embarrassing!' Hannah still went red at the thought.

Twenty-four hours after the helicopter had lifted her off the fell, she was out of hospital and heading for home. But her mum and dad had agreed to call in at Stonelea on the way.

'Never mind embarrassing. We were on the TV!' Helen boasted. 'They showed us on the local news!'

'Twins in Heroic Mercy Mission to Save Lost Kitten!' David laughed. 'That's my girls! In any case, that's what the Mountain Rescue team is for; to rescue people from mountains!'

'Er, I thought our plan was to give Helen and Hannah a severe talking to!' Mary reminded him. But a smile was playing around the corners of her own mouth. 'No more running off up mountains during a rainstorm; that kind of thing.'

'Of course, that is very important,' Lucy said, her face serious. She sat in her cane chair with Sheba on her lap and Mac curled up cosily alongside.

'We didn't know it was going to rain!' Helen

defended what they'd done. 'All we knew was that Mac was climbing the mountain and we had to try and stop him!'

'Which you did.' Mary agreed to let the matter drop. 'And I suppose we must be grateful that Hannah didn't do anything worse than bruise herself and sprain her ankle.'

'It's bad enough!' Hannah tried to raise her bandaged ankle from the floor, but groaned with pain. '. . . What?' she muttered to Helen, who had eyed her suspiciously.

'Nothing!' Helen hissed, with a look that said, *Don't you dare!*

Hannah stared back wide-eyed, then changed the subject to the reason for their visit. 'How's Mac?' she asked Lucy.

'Fortunately, Mac is none the worse for his adventure.' The Cat Lady tickled the kitten behind his ears and smiled fondly at him. 'I've given him a good talking-to and told Sheba to keep a close eye on him in future.'

Helen went over to Lucy's chair and stooped to pick Mac up. 'Can I?'

'Uhhh!' Hannah moaned, gritting her teeth.

'Dad, could you please bring that little stool for me to rest my foot on?'

David did as she asked with a thoughtful look.

'Who's a bad boy?' Helen held Mac up high and pretended to scold him. 'Who's a naughty kitten?'

Mac wriggled helplessly. When Helen lowered him to the floor, he scooted off under the kitchen table.

'Ohh, my ankle!' Hannah sighed.

In a flash, Mac dodged Lucy's two Persians, leaped over Tabs, performed a high-speed turn and wove his way back towards Hannah's chair.

'Is it really hurting?' Mary asked Hannah in a worried voice.

'Really, really!' she groaned. 'Honest, Mum, I don't think I'll be able to go to school tomorrow! In fact, I think I should stay here at Lucy's for a few days!'

'Hah!' Helen had known what was coming. ' "Honest, Mum!" ' she mocked behind Hannah's back.

'Hmm.' Mary looked at David, who seemed not to know what to say.

Neeyaah! Mac took another bend to avoid Hannah's sticking-out foot. He misjudged the curve and banged into the stool.

'Ah, poor Mac!' Forgetting to yelp, Hannah jumped up onto her one good foot. She bend down with a nimble movement to pick the dazed kitten off the floor.

'Hmm!' Mary said again, raising an eyebrow.

A broad smile spread across Helen's face. *Tough luck, Hann!*

'Ouch!' Hannah remembered and pretended to double up in pain.

Her mum and dad came up close to stroke and

comfort Mac. 'About school . . .' they began.

Hannah looked hopeful, but Helen knew she'd given herself away.

'Your mother and I have already discussed it,' David told her. 'And we do think you should have a couple of days off to rest your ankle.'

'B-b-but!' Helen was stunned.

'Quite right,' Lucy agreed. 'It's the least you deserve after what you went through for Mac!'

'Great!' Hannah sank down, relieved, in her chair, with the gorgeous black kitten, and gave a happy sigh. *No SCHOOL!*

'W-what about me?' Helen stammered. 'I might have caught hypo . . . hypother . . . I might have frozen to death on that mountain!'

'Nice try, Helen!' Her dad grinned. 'But it's only September; people don't die of cold unless it's winter. And the fact is, you're right as – well, right as rain!'

'Uhh!' Helen tried a groan, followed by a rough, choking cough. She collapsed into a spare chair and tried to look pale.

'SCHOOL!' her mum insisted.

'SCHOOL!' David echoed.

'So much for being a hero!' Helen grumbled, giving Hannah and Mac black looks. 'That's the last time I chase a cat up a mountain, OK?'